To:

From:

To my biggest supporters of whatever I do in life,

a.k.a

The Knebel Team!

SAM IS STUCK

THE KENTS' QUEST #1
Edition 4

by C. Knebel
Simple Words Books™

FREE DECODABLE
PHONICS WORKBOOK
and
FREE ACCESS TO ONLINE SUMMITS

simplewordsbooks.com

Chapter 1

The Day Of The Trip

It is the last Sunday in May. In spring, the Kents go on a day trip at a big pond. Tim's dad, Tom Kent, rents a ship for a day. The trips are a lot of fun.

It is the day of the big trip on the ship. On a hot spring day like this, it is not bad to be at the pond.

Tim is ten. He is tall and fit. He likes quests and hunts. There are a lot of quests and trash hunts on these trips.

"What will be the thrill on this trip?" Tim thinks.

Tim has his swim trunks on. He stuffs a red cap and sunblock in his bag. Then he zips it all the way. Tim has all he needs in the bag. He picks up his bag. He runs down the steps and out to the truck where his dad is.

Mr. Kent sets the bags in the back of the truck. Tim helps out his dad to prep for the trip.

"Tim, the bug spray kit is still in the shed. There will be a lot of bugs at the pond. We will need the kit with us on the trip. Can you  pick it up?" asks Mr. Kent. "Oh, and the net as well. I bet you will hunt for trash from the deck of the ship," he adds.

Tim nods. He thinks the trash hunt is the best job on the ship. It is fun to help the pond stay fresh.

Tim runs to the brick shed. He gets the bug kit from the shelf. He packs it in a box. On his way out, he grabs the net and sprints back to the truck.

The net is to pick the trash out of the pond. The net and the box go in the trunk of the truck.

All is set. It is time for Tim and his dad to go to the docks. They get in the truck.

"I am glad that we are on our way at last," Tim says to his dad with a big grin.

At the docks, Tim's dad stops the truck on a grass lot next to a fish hut. He runs into the hut and gets a ball of thick string.

"We must have string with us on the ship for the sling," he tells Tim.

Then they grab the bags, the net and the box with the bug kit. They bring them to the ship. Tim helps his dad get the ship set for the trip

The ship is small. It is black with a tint of red. A big flag hangs on the mast. There is a grill on the deck for lunch, a bench to sit on and a fan to chill the hot day. There is a rug in front of the fan. A cot is on the rug. The ship has all they will need for the day.

The sun is up at the top. It is a hot day. Tim does not want to get a tan.

He gets his red cap on and has sunblock on his skin. Then he looks back at the grass lot.

"When will they get to the docks?" he thinks as he looks for his mom and Kim.

Kim and Tim are siblings. Kim is six. She is not as tall as Tim. She has a pink dress and a black hat on. She has her best doll, Beck, in her hand.

Kim is in the van with her mom, Mrs. Kent. They went to the bank in the mall. Mrs. Kent got cash to pay for the vet visit.

On the way out of the mall, Mrs. Kent drops a $10 bill. Kim picks it up. She hands it back to her mom. Mrs. Kent lets Kim have the cash.

"I am rich," Kim grins to her mom.

"Last stop is the vet to pick up Bud," says Kim's mom.

Bud is Tim and Kim's pup. He is small and gray with black spots. When Bud is well, he runs and hops. When he is sick, he just sits on Kim's lap.

Bud was sick. He got a pill from the vet. The vet kept him for a day to check on him.

When Kim and her mom get to the vet, Bud jumps on Kim and licks her hand.

"Bud must be well," Kim tells her mom.

Mrs. Kent nods as she pets Bud's back. "Oh, Kim. We forgot to get snacks for Bud. This will be the last stop, O.K.?"

Kim grins. "Last stop. Then to the docks!"

Kim and Mrs. Kent go to a shop to get a box of snacks for Bud. Bud sits in the van. In the shop, Kim picks up snacks and a ball for Bud to play with. Mrs. Kent picks up bags of chips, nuts and figs for the kids. She grabs a box of milk from the shelf to drink on the trip.

Kim picks up a mint gum at the checkout. Mrs. Kent is all set to pay. But she does not have her bag. She had left it in the van. She has no cash with her.

Kim helps her mom pay for the snacks with the $10 bill she got from her mom in the mall. It is fun for Kim to help her mom when she is in need. But she has no cash left on her for the mint gum. She sets the gum back on the shelf.

"Oh, well," she thinks. "I will get the gum next time."

Kim and Mrs. Kent bring the bags to the van. It is time to go to the docks. When they get to the docks, they stop the van next to Mr. Kent's truck on the grass. Kim jumps out of the van.

Mrs. Kent has so much in her hands to bring to the ship. She drops a bag on the grass. Kim runs back to help her. She picks up the bag. Then, she sprints to the ship.

At last, they are on the docks. Kim, her mom and Bud spot Tim and Mr. Kent on the ship. They run up the ramp and hop on the ship.

Bud is glad to be on the ship with the kids. He is quick to jump on  Tim. He licks his hand as well. Tim hugs the pup and pets his neck.

The Kents are set for the trip. It is time to go. The ship is off the dock.

Flocks of ducks rush off from the pond next to the ship. Off they go on a quest as well. Just like Tim and Kim.

"I can tell this will be a fun day for all," Tim thinks with a grin.

Chapter 2

On The Ship

It is a fresh day. There is no wind, just the mist. The ship rocks on the pond.

Mr. and Mrs. Kent stand at the front of the deck. Mr. Kent was spot on. There are a lot of bugs on the pond. Mrs. Kent gets the bug spray out of the box. They all spray their skin.

Tim brings out the
net to hunt for trash. He
stands on the front deck
with Kim. He does not
spot any trash in the pond.

Then the kids go to the back of the
ship. And there is no trash at the back.
Tim is glad for that. But he is sad the
hunt ends so fast.

Tim dips his hand in the pond.

"Brrr. It is a hot day. But it is just
spring. It is still not hot in the pond.
I do not want to swim. I will not get
wet," he tells Kim. "I do not want to
get sick."

Kim nods. She will not dip in the pond. Just like Tim, she has no plans to get wet. She sits on the bench by the fan and plays with Beck to kill time. The wind from the fan chills her on this hot day.

Kim hugs Beck and then sets her on the bench next to her. She gets a big cup of milk to drink. The cup has a black lid. She casts the lid in the trash bin next to the bench.

Kim sips her drink. She sets the cup of milk on top of the tin chest next to the bench. But the lid is not on the cup. It is in the trash.

Tim grabs the bag with the snacks. He sits down on the bench next to Kim. He snacks on nuts. He splits a nut in half. Half is for Tim. Half is for Kim.

"We got chips in the bag as well," says Kim. She gets the bag of chips out. She checks the rest of the snacks.

"What is that?" she asks.

Tim looks in the bag.

"They are figs," Tim says. "Do you want it?" he asks.

"Yuck!" says Kim.

"Hmm. Yum," hints Tim. He hands a fig to Kim.

Kim tests the fig. Yum. "Oh, I like figs," she tells Tim.

"New things can be fun," adds Tim with a grin.

Bud rests on the cot in front of the fan. He looks like a rich king as he naps in the sun.

Bud is not fed yet. When he smells his snacks, he jumps off the cot. He does not want to be left out. He sprints fast to get a snack. But he bumps into Kim.

Kim falls off the bench and lands flat on her back. Her milk spills on the deck and her dress gets wet.

"Oh, I need a bib," kids Kim. "Glad I have my bikini on."

Tim is quick. He runs to get a rag and mops the mess off the deck. Not a drop is left on the deck.

Kim sits back on the bench. But Beck is not there.

"Oh, no!" she gasps. "Where is Beck?"

Tim checks the pond. He looks to his left. Beck drifts on the pond.

"Beck is in the pond. I think she fell in when you fell off the bench," yells Tim. "But she did not sink yet. I can fish her out. Get the net. Be quick!"

Kim hands the net to Tim. He gets Beck out of the pond fast. Kim grabs her from the net. She hugs her. Then, she hugs Tim.

Tim sits back on the bench to rest. Just as he sips his milk, a fish taps on the hull of the ship. The fish is big and flat.

The fish looks up at Tim and says, "I am Gup, the Ray Fish."

Chapter 3

A Fish Wish

"Can you help my pal, Sam, the Cod Fish? He is stuck in a rock down in the pond," Gup says.

Tim sprays his milk.

"What was that? What did you say? Are you a fish?" he asks.

Kim checks out the fish as well. "Is this a spell? Oh, pinch me. Are you a fish or… or…" That is all she can say.

In shock, Tim yells, "Mom!" and Kim yells, "Dad!"

Bud jumps up and down on the deck. He yaps and yaps at the fish.

Mr. and Mrs. Kent rush to the back of the ship. "Are you O.K., kids?" Mr. Kent asks. Mrs. Kent hugs them. Tim tells his mom and dad that he just met a fish and it needs his help.

They step to the brink of the ship. The fish is still by the plank.

"Can I go with
Gup to help his pal,
Sam?" asks Tim.

"Can I go with them as well?" asks
Kim.

Mr. and Mrs. Kent nod. They jot
down a list of things the kids can and
cannot do in the pond. They want no
risk to the kids.

Mr. Kent hands the kids the thick
string he got at the fish hut for the
sling. He clips the end of the string to
a bell on the ship. This string will be
the kids' link to the ship when they
are down in the pond.

"Just yank the string to ring the bell if you need help," tells Mr. Kent to Kim and Tim.

"And do not split up in the pond. Got it?" adds Mrs. Kent.

Tim and Kim nod. They strap the string to their hips. They rush to get into the pond. But they stop and run back. They hug their mom and dad.

Then they hop on the plank. They forget that the pond is not hot. Kim grabs Tim's hand. They jump into the pond with a big splash.

Tim and Kim are on a quest now.

This is a big task. They rush to help Gup and his pal, Sam.

Tim and Kim like to swim with Gup. This is a big thrill! And it is a lot of fun.

Tim and Gup swim fast. But Kim is not as quick as they are. So she grabs on to Tim's hand.

As Gup swims down with the kids, he stops to ask, "Do you want to rest? We can stop for a bit."

Tim checks on Kim. She asks when they will get to Sam. Gup checks his map. Then, he hands the map to Tim with his small fin.

Tim scans the map. There is a big red dot on the map. This is where Sam is.

"It is still a bit until we get to Sam," says Tim. "Do you want to rest, Kim?" he asks.

Kim says no.

"Then let us just go on," says Tim.

They swim past the jellyfish and check out the clams.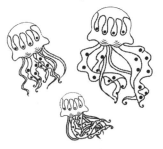

Tim spots a small shell on the crest of a hill in the pond. The shell glints in the sun. He picks up the shell  and sticks it in his pocket. He plans to gift the shell to his mom and dad when he is back on the ship.

Gup chats with the kids as they swim. He tells how he spends his days in the pond with his best pal, Sam.

In the nick of time, Gup says, "Hush! Hush! Stop!" He lifts his left fin up. A big gray fish is next to them.

It is a shark! It
blocks the way for
them. It has big
black gills. Its lips
are red. Tim and
Kim look at Gup to check if he is O.K.
Tim swims back and stands still. The
shark does not pick up on them and
swims out of the way.

Kim asks, "Are we there yet?"

Tim checks the map and says, "Yes!"

Gup yells, "There is my best pal!"

There is Sam.

Chapter 4

Sam The Cod Fish

Sam, the Cod Fish, is a small fish. He is stuck in a gap in the rocks. What are the odds of that?

"Rush, rush, rush. Let us help him out. Be quick!" yells Gup.

Kim swims to Sam.

"Hi. I am Kim," she says.

"And I am Tim," Tim adds.

Kim gasps, "How did you fit in that small pit? How can we get you out of this gap?"

"Do not fret," says Tim. "Sam will be out of this pit in no time."

"Hi, Kim. Hi, Tim. I am Sam," says Sam. He does not say a thing more.

He is sad and he cannot mask it. This is not fun for him. It looks like he is out of gas.

Tim pats Sam on the chin. He checks the rocks. They are set in the thick mud. He asks Sam how he got stuck in the rocks.

"It was lunch time. I left my pals at camp and snuck out. I went out for a swim. But I did not tell my pals or Mr. Shrimp that I left. Mr. Shrimp runs the camp. It was bad that I left with no pass from him. I swam and swam. Then I got lost. I did not bring my

map. I left it back at the camp. The sun went down and it got dim in the pond. I did not spot the rocks. Then BAMMM!! I got stuck in this small crack. This is a big mess. All bad luck," Sam tells the kids.

"Bad luck or a bad plan? What do you think?" asks Gup with a grin.

"I was not there when you swam out of the camp," he adds. "Mr. Shrimp was upset that you left the camp with no pass. And no map. The sun went down. When it was up, you were still not back. Then I got a pass from Mr. Shrimp. I swam to look for you. And there you were. Stuck in the rocks."

"I will not swim off like that next time," says Sam. Then he asks Tim and Kim, "Do you think you can help me get out of this mess?" His lips are still down. He wants to be back at the camp and play with his pals.

"We are glad we met Gup," says Kim. "We will help you. Mom and Dad are on the ship. They can help as well."

"We can fix this for you," Tim says. "You are in the best hands."

Sam thinks there may be a way out. He is not as sad as he was when they met.

Kim kicks the big rock. No luck. It is as if the rock is a ton.

They bang.

They slam.

But still no luck. The rock is still stuck in the thick mud.

"Hang in there, Sam. Do not be upset," says Tim. He thinks they can get Sam out of the pit. "We will get you out in no time. Trust me on this."

Time ticks by. But there is still no hint of a plan. Tim rubs his chin.

Then he says, "I bet there is a way. But it stinks that I cannot tell what it is. Let us think step by step."

What can they do to get Sam out of this pit?

Chapter 5

The Grand Plan

There must be a way to get Sam out of this rock. Yet, there is still not a hint of a plan. This is bad. And it bugs Tim a lot.

"I want to shred this rock!" Tim says with a grunt.

Kim asks, "Can we chop the rock into bits?"

"Well, the rock is big. We can chip it, but not chop it," says Tim.

"Can we dig it out?" asks Kim.

Then it hits him. This may be just the plan they need.

"Yes, Kim. We can dig the rock out," says Tim. "Then, Sam will be out of the pit."

Tim and Kim go for it. They dig and dig with their hands. But that does not do the trick. This is still a no go.

The plan to dig out the rock was not bad. But they need to edit it a bit. The mud is too thick to dig by hand.

"Do you still think you can do this, Tim?" asks Sam.

"Yes, we can! We can dig this rock out," says Tim. "This is a big job. We just need to shift the way we think."

Kim swims up and down a bit. Then she says, "What if we get a stick. A stick may help us dig out the rock."

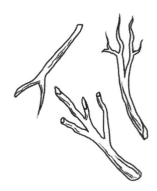

"You bet it will!" says Tim. "You have the best plans on this trip, Kim."

"Not just a hat rack, Tim," Kim says with a grin. This is what her dad says when he has a grand plan.

"We got the best plan, let us vet it out. Where can we get a bunch of sticks in the pond?" asks Tim.

Gup jumps in the chat, "There are sticks off the cliff to the left."

Tim asks Gup, "May I send you to pick up a bunch of them?"

"Yes! Yes! Yes! I can get them for you! I will be back in a flash," says

Gup. He is glad to help. He zigs and zags and gets a lot of sticks.

In a blink, Gup is back with a stack of sticks. Kim picks up a stick to test it. She lifts it up and acts as if she digs in the mud. The stick bends and cracks. It slips out of her hand and hits Tim's leg.

"Aww!" sobs Tim. His skin gets red.

Kim hugs him. Tim hugs her back as he rubs his leg.

"I am O.K.," Tim tells Kim. But he limps a bit. "It is just a small bump. I am not cut. Do not be upset," he adds.

"The string is not cut. We still got the link to the ship. Let us get back to the task. We will bring this quest to an end."

The kids lay the bunch of sticks on the sand. They sift out the bad sticks. They dump all but the big and thick sticks. They will dig with the best.

And that is what they do. They dig and dig. It is not much until the rock is out.

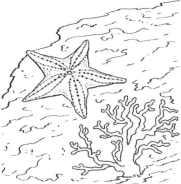

"Do not stop now. Just a bit left. Let us fix

this thing! Let us finish this job!" says
Tim to all.

At last, there is a big crack! The
rock pops out and falls down the hill.

"We did it! We did it!" yells the
gang.

Sam is out!

Chapter 6

The Quest Ends

Sam swims out of the pit. He is glad. They are all glad. They jump up and down. They all clap and splash.

"Let us exit this spot. Let us swim back up to the ship," says Tim.

They all grab the string and yank it. Mr. and Mrs. Kent stand by the string on the deck. When the bell rings on the ship, they tug the string up fast.

Tim, Kim, Sam and Gup swim back up to the top with the help of the string.

Mr. Kent grabs Tim's and Kim's hands. The kids jump on the ship.

Mrs. Kent picks up Sam out of the pond with the net. She brings him to a big fish tank on the deck to rest for a bit. Gup stays in the pond.

Mrs. Kent checks on Sam.

"Does he need a vet?" Kim asks her mom.

"No," says Mrs. Kent. "All he needs is a bit of rest. He will be back in the pond with his pal Gup, the Ray Fish, in no time," she adds.

Sam stays in the tank. He mends as the ship sets back for the docks.

Gup still swims by the ship.

It is way past lunch time. Mr. Kent and Mrs. Kent chop buns and mix them with eggs in a pan on the grill.

The kids gulp down their lunch. They run to the back of the ship to check on Sam. He looks well.

Kim brings out the ball from the bag. She casts the ball to pass time. Bud runs and gets the ball. He brings it back to Kim. Kim rubs Bud's back. Bud likes this a lot. Beck sits on the bench, out of the way.

Tim spends the rest of the trip, or what is left of it, on the deck. But he does not play with Kim and Bud. He rests on the cot. He has much to think of.

"What a day this was," thinks Tim. "There is no limit to what I can do when I do not quit. When I go for it with all I got. Just like I did down in the pond. I will not let things get to me. I will do my best."

The sun sets. The flocks of ducks are back from their quest as well. They rest on the pond. It is time for them to go back to their nests.

Tim thinks of the shell he got in the pond. It is still in his pocket. "Mom and Dad were there to help," he thinks.

His mom and dad are on the deck. Mrs. Kent sits next to Mr. Kent on the bench. Tim runs to them. He gets the shell out of his pocket.

"Mom! Dad! I have a small gift for you as a thank you for all you do for me."

He sets the shell in his mom's hand. "A shell to think of this trip, Sam and Gup. And me."

Mr. and Mrs. Kent hug Tim and say, "This shell will bring us luck."

"The sunset was not like the rest of the days," says Tim with a wish that his mom and dad get what he says.

Mrs. Kent nods.

"I get that, Son. I felt that way as well," says Mr. Kent. "Some days are just like that. They shift the way we think. Then on, things are not as they were in the past. In fact, these days imprint who we are. This trip was like that for you. I am glad that I was there with you on a day like this. And I am glad to be your dad."

Mrs. Kent gets up to check on Sam. Kim and Tim are glad that Sam is well.

"He can go back to the pond and be with his pal," she says to the kids.

They look in the pond. Gup still hangs out by the ship.

Mr. Kent helps Sam get back in the pond. Gup is glad to be with his best pal. Kim and Tim are a bit sad to let Sam go. They wish for him to be with them until the day ends. But they want the best for him. And they can tell it is time for him to go back in the pond to be with his fish pals.

"I wish you a fun trip on your way back," yells Tim.

"We will miss you!" adds Kim.

This is the end of Tim and Kim's quest. The quest and the trip end well.

Sam, the Cod Fish, swims into the sunset with Gup, the Ray Fish. He and his best pal are off to their next quest.

You can download full color

CERTIFICATE OF ACCOMPLISHMENT
and
CERTIFICATE OF COMPLETION

On our website

SIMPLEWORDSBOOKS.COM

Certificate of Accomplishment

This certificate is awarded to

_____

for successful completion of

Sam Is Stuck

_____   _____
Signature   Date

SIMPLE WORDS

SAM IS STUCK

WORD LIST

#	Word	Count	#	Word	Count	#	Word	Count
1	a	121	26	bench	12	51	bunch	3
2	acts	1	27	bends	1	52	buns	1
3	adds	8	28	best	12	53	but	21
4	all	17	29	bet	3	54	by	8
5	am	10	30	bib	1	55	camp	6
6	an	1	31	big	19	56	can	28
7	and	112	32	bikini	1	57	cannot	3
8	any	1	33	bill	2	58	cap	2
9	are	32	34	bin	1	59	cash	4
10	as	27	35	bit	9	60	casts	2
11	ask	1	36	bits	1	61	chat	1
12	asks	19	37	black	5	62	chats	1
13	at	19	38	blink	1	63	check	5
14	aww	1	39	blocks	1	64	checkout	1
15	back	36	40	box	6	65	checks	8
16	bad	8	41	brick	1	66	chest	1
17	bag	11	42	bring	6	67	chill	1
18	bags	4	43	brings	4	68	chills	1
19	ball	5	44	brink	1	69	chin	2
20	bammm	1	45	brrr	1	70	chip	1
21	bang	1	46	Bud	20	71	chips	3
22	bank	1	47	bug	4	72	chop	3
23	be	27	48	bugs	3	73	clams	1
24	Beck	9	49	bump	1	74	clap	1
25	bell	3	50	bumps	1	75	cliff	1

#	Word	Count	#	Word	Count	#	Word	Count
76	clips	1	101	dress	2	126	fix	2
77	cod	3	102	drifts	1	127	flag	1
78	cot	4	103	drink	3	128	flash	1
79	crack	2	104	drop	1	129	flat	2
80	cracks	1	105	drops	2	130	flocks	2
81	crest	1	106	ducks	2	131	for	44
82	cup	4	107	dump	1	132	forget	1
83	cut	2	108	edit	1	133	forgot	1
84	dad	18	109	eggs	1	134	fresh	2
85	day	15	110	end	4	135	fret	1
86	days	4	111	ends	2	136	from	12
87	deck	12	112	exit	1	137	front	4
88	did	9	113	fact	1	138	fun	8
89	dig	11	114	falls	2	139	gang	1
90	digs	1	115	fan	5	140	gap	2
91	dim	1	116	fast	5	141	gas	1
92	dip	1	117	fed	1	142	gasps	2
93	dips	1	118	fell	2	143	get	32
94	do	22	119	felt	1	144	gets	13
95	dock	1	120	fig	2	145	gift	2
96	docks	8	121	figs	3	146	gills	1
97	does	9	122	fin	2	147	glad	12
98	doll	1	123	finish	1	148	glints	1
99	dot	1	124	fish	22	149	go	18
100	down	15	125	fit	2	150	got	15

#	Word	Count	#	Word	Count	#	Word	Count
151	grab	2	176	hi	3	201	is	114
152	grabs	7	177	hill	2	202	it	64
153	grand	1	178	him	11	203	its	1
154	grass	4	179	hint	2	204	jellyfish	1
155	gray	2	180	hints	1	205	job	3
156	grill	2	181	hips	1	206	jot	1
157	grin	5	182	his	45	207	jump	4
158	grins	2	183	hits	2	208	jumps	5
159	grunt	1	184	hmm	1	209	just	16
160	gulp	1	185	hop	2	210	Kent	39
161	gum	4	186	hops	1	211	Kents	2
162	Gup	27	187	hot	7	212	kept	1
163	had	1	188	how	4	213	kicks	1
164	half	3	189	hug	2	214	kids	16
165	hand	9	190	hugs	7	215	kill	1
166	hands	9	191	hull	1	216	Kim	84
167	hang	1	192	hunt	4	217	king	1
168	hangs	2	193	hunts	2	218	kit	4
169	has	14	194	hush	2	219	lands	1
170	hat	2	195	hut	3	220	lap	1
171	have	6	196	I	56	221	last	7
172	he	99	197	if	5	222	lay	1
173	help	16	198	imprint	1	223	left	14
174	helps	4	199	in	75	224	leg	2
175	her	31	200	into	6	225	let	11

#	Word	Count
226	lets	1
227	licks	2
228	lid	3
229	lifts	2
230	like	13
231	likes	2
232	limit	1
233	limps	1
234	link	2
235	lips	2
236	list	1
237	look	3
238	looks	8
239	lost	1
240	lot	10
241	luck	5
242	lunch	4
243	mall	3
244	map	7
245	mask	1
246	mast	1
247	may	5
248	me	6
249	mends	1
250	mess	3

#	Word	Count
251	met	3
252	milk	6
253	mint	2
254	miss	1
255	mist	1
256	mix	1
257	mom	22
258	mops	1
259	more	1
260	Mr.	22
261	Mrs.	25
262	much	3
263	mud	4
264	must	3
265	my	7
266	naps	1
267	neck	1
268	need	9
269	needs	3
270	nests	1
271	net	10
272	new	1
273	next	12
274	nick	1
275	no	20

#	Word	Count
276	nod	2
277	nods	4
278	not	46
279	now	2
280	nut	1
281	nuts	2
282	O.K.	4
283	odds	1
284	of	70
285	off	10
286	oh	7
287	on	87
288	or	5
289	our	1
290	out	46
291	packs	1
292	pal	9
293	pals	4
294	pan	1
295	pass	4
296	past	3
297	pats	1
298	pay	3
299	pets	2
300	pick	5

#	Word	Count	#	Word	Count	#	Word	Count
301	picks	9	326	rest	9	351	shelf	3
302	pill	1	327	rests	2	352	shell	9
303	pinch	1	328	rich	2	353	shift	2
304	pink	1	329	ring	1	354	ship	33
305	pit	6	330	rings	1	355	shock	1
306	plan	7	331	risk	1	356	shop	2
307	plank	2	332	rock	14	357	shred	1
308	plans	3	333	rocks	6	358	shrimp	4
309	play	3	334	rubs	3	359	siblings	1
310	plays	1	335	rug	2	360	sick	3
311	pocket	3	336	run	3	361	sift	1
312	pond	37	337	runs	9	362	sink	1
313	pops	1	338	rush	7	363	sips	2
314	prep	1	339	sad	4	364	sit	1
315	pup	2	340	Sam	37	365	sits	8
316	quest	7	341	sand	1	366	six	1
317	quests	2	342	say	4	367	skin	3
318	quick	5	343	says	36	368	slam	1
319	quit	1	344	scans	1	369	sling	2
320	rack	1	345	send	1	370	slips	1
321	rag	1	346	set	5	371	small	9
322	ramp	1	347	sets	7	372	smells	1
323	ray	3	348	shark	2	373	snack	1
324	red	6	349	she	43	374	snacks	8
325	rents	1	350	shed	2	375	snuck	1

#	Word	Count	#	Word	Count	#	Word	Count
376	so	3	401	still	17	426	thank	1
377	sobs	1	402	stinks	1	427	that	23
378	some	1	403	stop	8	428	the	360
379	son	1	404	stops	2	429	their	8
380	spell	1	405	strap	1	430	them	12
381	spends	2	406	string	12	431	then	20
382	spills	1	407	stuck	6	432	there	25
383	splash	2	408	stuffs	1	433	these	2
384	split	1	409	sun	6	434	they	57
385	splits	1	410	sunblock	2	435	thick	6
386	spot	5	411	sunday	1	436	thing	2
387	spots	2	412	sunset	2	437	things	4
388	spray	3	413	swam	4	438	think	9
389	sprays	1	414	swim	10	439	thinks	10
390	spring	3	415	swims	8	440	this	40
391	sprints	3	416	tall	2	441	thrill	2
392	stack	1	417	tan	1	442	ticks	1
393	stand	2	418	tank	2	443	Tim	99
394	stands	2	419	taps	1	444	time	16
395	stay	1	420	task	2	445	tin	1
396	stays	2	421	tell	4	446	tint	1
397	step	3	422	tells	9	447	to	130
398	steps	1	423	ten	1	448	Tom	1
399	stick	4	424	test	1	449	ton	1
400	sticks	8	425	tests	1	450	too	1

#	Word	Count
451	top	3
452	trash	9
453	trick	1
454	trip	14
455	trips	2
456	truck	7
457	trunk	1
458	trunks	1
459	trust	1
460	tug	1
461	until	3
462	up	27
463	upset	3
464	us	13
465	van	6
466	vet	7
467	visit	1
468	want	10
469	wants	1
470	was	14
471	way	15
472	we	32
473	well	16
474	went	4
475	were	4

#	Word	Count
476	wet	3
477	what	15
478	when	18
479	where	4
480	who	1
481	will	27
482	wind	2
483	wish	3
484	with	46
485	yank	2
486	yaps	2
487	yells	7
488	yes	6
489	yet	4
490	you	39
491	your	2
492	yuck	1
493	yum	2
494	zags	1
495	zigs	1
496	zips	1
Total Words		**4351**

SAM IS STUCK

COMPREHENSION WORKBOOK

CH 1-1. What is the big event of the day?

_____

_____

_____

_____

_____

_____

_____

_____

_____

_____

_____

_____

_____

_____

_____

_____

_____

_____

CH 1-2. Can you describe Tim? How old is he? How does he look? What does he wear?

_____

_____

_____

_____

_____

_____

_____

_____

_____

_____

_____

_____

_____

_____

_____

_____

_____

_____

_____

CH 1-3. What are the things Kim and Mrs. Kent buy in the shop?

_____

_____

_____

_____

_____

_____

_____

_____

_____

_____

_____

_____

_____

_____

_____

_____

_____

_____

_____

CH 1-4. Why does Kim pay for the things Mrs. Kent picked up in the store?

_____

_____

_____

_____

_____

_____

_____

_____

_____

_____

_____

_____

_____

_____

_____

_____

_____

_____

CH 2-1. Why do Tim and Kim not want to swim today?

_____

_____

_____

_____

_____

_____

_____

_____

_____

_____

_____

_____

_____

_____

_____

_____

_____

_____

_____

_____

CH 2-2. What are the kids snacking on?

_____

_____

_____

_____

_____

_____

_____

_____

_____

_____

_____

_____

_____

_____

_____

_____

_____

_____

_____

CH 2-3. Why does Bud bump into Kim?

_____

_____

_____

_____

_____

_____

_____

_____

_____

_____

_____

_____

_____

_____

_____

_____

_____

_____

_____

_____

CH 2-4. What happens in Chapter 2 that will not happen in real life?

_____

_____

_____

_____

_____

_____

_____

_____

_____

_____

_____

_____

_____

_____

_____

_____

_____

_____

CH 3-1.Why are Tim and Kim surprised?

CH 3-2.Who will help Sam?

CH 3-3.What is the kids' link to the ship?

_____

_____

_____

_____

_____

_____

_____

_____

_____

_____

_____

_____

_____

_____

_____

_____

_____

_____

_____

_____

CH 3-4. What does Tim see in the water as they swim to Sam?

_____

_____

_____

_____

_____

_____

_____

_____

_____

_____

_____

_____

_____

_____

_____

_____

_____

_____

_____

CH 4-1.Why does Sam need help?

_____

_____

_____

_____

_____

_____

_____

_____

_____

_____

_____

_____

_____

_____

_____

_____

_____

_____

_____

_____

CH 4-2.How did Sam get to the rocks?

CH 4-3.What do the kids use to move the rocks?

_____

_____

_____

_____

_____

_____

_____

_____

_____

_____

_____

_____

_____

_____

_____

_____

_____

_____

_____

CH 4-4.How does Tim feel at the end of this chapter? Why?

_____

_____

_____

_____

_____

_____

_____

_____

_____

_____

_____

_____

_____

_____

_____

_____

_____

_____

CH 5-1.What is the Grand Plan?

CH 5-2.Why is Gup glad to bring the sticks?

CH 5-3.Describe how the sticks Tim and Kim pick look.

_____

_____

_____

_____

_____

_____

_____

_____

_____

_____

_____

_____

_____

_____

_____

_____

_____

_____

_____

_____

CH 5-4.How does Tim get hurt? How does Kim feel about this? Why?

_____

_____

_____

_____

_____

_____

_____

_____

_____

_____

_____

_____

_____

_____

_____

_____

_____

_____

_____

CH 6-1.How do they all feel? Why?

_____

_____

_____

_____

_____

_____

_____

_____

_____

_____

_____

_____

_____

_____

_____

_____

_____

_____

_____

_____

_____

_____

CH 6-2. Who gets on the ship after they swim up? Name all.

_____

_____

_____

_____

_____

_____

_____

_____

_____

_____

_____

_____

_____

_____

_____

_____

_____

_____

_____

CH 6-3. Double dip feelings are having contradictory emotions. Who has double feelings in this chapter? How do they feel?

_____

_____

_____

_____

_____

_____

_____

_____

_____

_____

_____

_____

_____

_____

_____

_____

_____

_____

_____

_____

_____

CH 6-4.Why is Mr. Kent proud of Tim?

Do you want to write your own story now?

Written by:

_____

_____

_____

_____

_____

_____

_____

_____

_____

_____

_____

_____

_____

_____

_____

_____

_____

_____

_____

_____

Do you want to draw your own story now?

Illustrated by:

WANT TO READ MORE
CHAPTER BOOKS

Spelling Pen in Elf Land
by C.Knebel

7000 Words

Spelling Pen
Red Obelisk
by C.Knebel

FOX HUNT
by Cigdem Knebel

The Gold of Black Rock Hill
by C. Knebel

Six Days at Camp
With Jack and Max
by Cigdem Knebel

Six Days at Camp
With Lin and Jill
by Cigdem Knebel

STUDY GUIDES
AND
HANDBOOKS

www.simplewordsbooks.com